LEE ALEXANDER

Echoes of Dark and Light

The Damien Blackwell Chronicles

Imprint—Virginia Beach, VA

ISBN: 979-8-9911360-2-0

Library of Congress Control Number: pending

Title: Echoes of Dark and Light: The Damien Blackwell Chronicles

Author: Lee Alexander

Digital distribution | 2025

Paperback | 2025

First edition

ISBN: 979-8-9911360-2-0

Cover art by Erin Watkin

This book was professionally typeset on Reedsy.
Find out more at reedsy.com

I dedicate this to all my fellow veterans and others who are dealing with their own demons.

;IGY6;

Also, to all those who help people who are suffering from mental health issues, you are more appreciated than you will ever know.

In the USA, help is available Speak with someone today call 988 Suicide and Crisis Lifeline

Veterans can also use the following online resource for chat https://www.veteranscrisisline.net

or text 838255

Outside the USA, please find your help resources and talk to someone

Acknowledgments

A book's cover is its first whisper to the world, a glimpse into the soul of the story within. For bringing that vision to life so brilliantly, I owe my deepest thanks to Erin Watkin of Wales, UK. Her extraordinary talent, boundless creativity, and a keen eye for detail have given this book a striking face that speaks volumes before a single page is turned. Erin, your artistry is nothing short of magical, and I am beyond grateful for your work.

For those who appreciate masterful design, be sure to check out her incredible portfolio on Instagram: @crisis_artz.

Thank you, Erin, for making this journey even more beautiful!

Chapter 1

As darkness swirled in around Damien, he felt as if he weighed nothing at all. His eyes were open, but all he could see was darkness. It looked as if he could see for miles, but there was nothing to see. With nothing evident, did it mean he had died in the fight? Did he fall unconscious but still win the fight? He felt a wave of pain come from his chest and felt himself lose consciousness again. Was this hope or hopelessness?

Damien's eyes opened again when he heard his dad's voice commanding him to get up and take a strong fighting position. He could feel the intensity and what seemed to be anger coming from his father. It all seemed so familiar but also unreal.

Damien's father, Arthor, yelled, "Get up, get your sword, and ready yourself!"

Damien struggled to his feet. He looked at his father and groggily said, "I am ready, father."

Arthor swung his sword, knocked Damien's sword from his hand, and said, "This is why you need to master the skill of sword fighting. Skill, wisdom, and dexterity will do you much better than strength. The Blood Bain Sword was created to damage the unholy with just a small cut of the flesh. It does not require strength and deep cuts."

Ten-year-old Damien looked at his father and said, "Did your strength knock the sword from my hand?"

His father looked deeply at him and said, "If your skills were more advanced, you would have parried, moved, and struck me on the side. Learn to see the next two moves you will make and learn your opponent's weaknesses."

Damien looked to the ground, feeling defeated, and said, "You have no weakness, Father."

Arthor looked at Damien, felt his sadness, and said, "We all have weaknesses, my son."

Arthor sheathed his sword, walked over to his son, and pulled him into a strong hug. Damien hugged

him back, looked up at his dad, smiled, and said, "I will make you proud one day, father."

Arthor looked into his son's eyes and smiled, "You already do, my son. Now, let's get something to eat."

Damien turned and picked his sword up off the ground, then turned back to follow his father with a renewed feeling of confidence. Just as he stepped toward his dad, everything went black again, and he thought, was that a dream, or am I just recalling moments from my life as I pass to the afterworld? He was still very uncertain if he was dead or alive.

In his thoughts were two realities working. One where he had died without an heir for the family name, along with an end to his cursed life. Another where he feared being dead with no heir to carry on his family legacy to continue to help those in need from the evils of the world. In one reality, he would gain peace and rest, and in the other, he would be tormented for eternity for the incomplete life he had left behind. Damien was also hopeful that a third possible reality existed where he was unconscious and could continue his legacy and have an heir to pass on the family name and birthright.

Damien's eyes shot open to the sound of clashing swords. In front of him was his father battling a demon, a familiar one. This was the battle when he saw his first real demon. His father battled Lazif when he was just a young boy. As he watched the blades arc through the air and smash against each other, he could hear the metal clank and sparks fly from the enchanted blades. Arthor and Lazif pushed in on one another, but Arthor was pushed back but did not lose his balance. A testament to the master swordsman he was.

Lazif quickly stepped towards Damien, grabbed him, and tossed him across the room. Young Damien was so scared he wet his pants and crashed into the furniture. He landed hard against a wooden chair, shattering it, and bounced off a bookshelf against the wall. The impact almost knocked him unconscious and knocked the wind out of his lungs, making him gasp for air. His eyes were only partly open, and it was hard to focus, but he saw his father bump between him and Lazif, landing a hard strike against Lazif. The blood spilled across the blade of the Blood Bain Sword and onto the floor. It looked to Damien as if less blood hit the floor than came from the demon's wound. Lazif stumbled back and took up a weakened defensive position, grasping his wound.

The sword in Arthor's hand began to glow red as he said what sounded to be a prayer, "Lumen ferox, excitare! Da mihi fortitudinem tuam et victoriam in tenebris!" (Translation:

"Fierce light, awaken! Grant me your strength and victory over the darkness!") Damien's father lunged forward and struck Lazif once again, and with that strike, he turned into a dark mist and was absorbed into the ground. Once again, everything went black.

Damien's mind raced with images from his life as if his entire existence had passed before him. His grandfather, father, teachers, friends, and colleagues all appeared in fleeting visions. Each flash felt like flipping through a photo album of never-taken pictures. Suddenly, the images stopped, and the memory that filled his mind was the first time he saw Vivian. He was looking at himself, looking at her. Their eyes seemed to look deep into each other's soul, and the smile on her face brought an overall feeling of elation to him. The joy Damien felt at that moment in time was one that he had only experienced when he first saw Vivian and every time he saw her after that.

Damien thought to himself that moment was the moment that would make an afterlife blissful and fulfilled. Nothing else in his life brought him a more euphoric feeling. Vivian: She was his happiness, his core memory that tied his life together, and the source of all things good in the world. Damien clung to her memory to guide him to whatever would come next. The memory of not just her beauty but her voice, her laughter, and her warm touch. It may be too late, but Damien realized that Vivian was not just his past and present – she was his eternity.

Chapter 2

When the sounds from inside the house ended in a loud, otherworldly scream, Vivian and everyone outside turned to the house and stood in silence with their eyes fixed on the front door. All of the people standing outside continued their prayers inside their heads, and Vivian could only keep thinking that Damien would walk through the door any second. Vivian stared hard at the door knob and tried to will Damien to open the door and return to her, no matter his condition, just alive. She held the antivenom she had created in her pocket, ready to administer it as soon as he opened the door.

Vivian unconsciously began to take small steps towards the door and contemplated opening the door to rush to Damien's aid. But she knew he would open the door with the child safe in his arms. For the first time in all the years she had known him, she could not sense his life force and did not know if he was alive or not. Her inner dialog was drowning out everything around her. She could see the vicar's mouth moving but could not hear any sounds. Her heart pounded, and her anxiety was almost overwhelming. After her slow walk to the door, which seemed to take hours, she gripped the door handle and pulled the key from her pocket. As she inserted and turned the key, her heart suddenly began to beat normally. Her instinct as a healer had taken over, and she had become equanimous and ready for the worst.

Vivian unlocked the door, turned the knob, and opened the door. The child's parents held their breath, and everyone stared at Vivian as she stepped into the house. Vivian jumped back as the young boy stumbled towards her and startled Vivian. She caught him as he began to fall at her feet. He was covered in blood, and Vivian's instincts kicked in, and she began to check him over. There were wounds all over his body, and he had lost a lot of blood, but he was breathing. Most of his breaths were short and quick, but he was alive!

Vivian called out, "He is alive! We need to get him cleaned up and work on these wounds."

She picked him up and took him over the table they had made into a makeshift healing station. The mother and father ran to help her carry him over to the table and gently laid him down. Vivian began to work on his more prominent wounds, and the nurse cleaned and dressed the smaller ones. His parents stood by his head, touching him and praying. Several wounds were sigils that the demons had carved into his skin, and as they worked on his wounds, Vivian took mental note of all the sigils. She recognized a few of them, making her want to run back into the house and find Damian even more.

The nurse, Sasha, touched Vivian's hand and said, "Go, find Damien. I can handle this."

Vivian looked up at her and said, "Thank you." She quickly

walked off into the house, and the vicar, along with two more sturdy men, walked right behind her.

As they walked through the house towards the boy's room, they saw the trail of blood from where he stumbled down the hallway. The door to the room stood open, and the entire contents of the room were piled against one wall as if thrown there. The foul stench of various body fluids filled the air, making them gag and cover their noses. Vivian began to step into the room, but the vicar stopped her and looked at the two men with them as if to say let them go first. She moved aside, and the men stepped through the door cautiously. She saw them both look to their left and move quickly out of sight. Vivian's heart sank.

One of the men, Hassan, called to Vivian, "Damien is here, and I don't think he is alive."

Vivian and the vicar quickly stepped through the door, and she ran to Damien's side as the vicar began to bless the room, just in case. Vivian felt faint but was not going to break down. This is what she was here for, and this is what she did best. There was no one else Damien trusted to heal him when needed, and she would not fail him. Her hands moved as if guided by something or someone else. Vivian applied everything she had brought to stabilize Damien, but her mind could hardly keep up with her hands. She knew she had done all she could right here and now, and she still could not sense his life force.

Vivian looked at the two men and said, "Can you move him to my home?"

Hassan nodded at Vivian and said, "We will move him to my horse cart just outside and take him to your home. You go and get in now; we will be right behind you."

Hassan then looked at Yusuf and said, "Sana'khudhuhu ila

arabat ḥiṣani thumma ila manzil al-mualij." (Transliteration: We will move him to my horse cart and take him to the healer's home.)

As Vivian left to get into Hassan's cart, the two men carefully lifted Damien, and Yusuf said, "Hal naqluhu hunak li-tastaṭee'a an tu'iddahu li-daftihi?" (Transliteration: Are we moving him there so she can prepare him for his burial?)

Hassan looked at him and responded, "Azhon innaha tumin innu ma zal hayyan." (Transliteration: I think she believes he is still alive.)

The men looked at each other disheartened and lifted Damien off the ground. As they began to carry him out of the room, the Vicar made the sign of the cross, picked Damien's sword up off the ground, and followed them. The people had lined up just outside the house and were beginning to chant prayers of healing and hope as Vivian walked out towards the horse cart.

Sasha approached her and said, "The boy is breathing strong now and should be well enough to wake up in a day or two. I should come with you."

Vivian squeezed her hand and said, "I am happy the boy is doing well. I don't think there is anything I can do for Damien. Why don't you stay and help the family."

Sasha put her other hand on top of Vivian's and said, "I will help get the boy settled where the family wants him to rest and be on my way to your home. With your healing skills and the love I see you have for him, there has to be something you can do. Don't give up on him yet."

Vivian forced a smile as she climbed into the cart and said, "Thank you. If you want to come to my home...........hartshorn. I have hartshorn at home."

Sasha smiled and said, "Do all you can, and I will be along

soon."

The men gently laid Damien in the cart and climbed in. Hassan reigned the horse to get him moving. They traveled quickly, and he tried to keep the cart as smooth as possible across the cobblestone street. Once they arrived, Vivian jumped from the cart, threw the door open, ran in, and began to mix a concoction of hartshorn, antiseptic alcohol, and peppermint. The men followed shortly behind her, carrying Damien.

Before the men could speak, Vivian said, "Lay him on this bed." She pointed at a bed without looking away from her work.

The men gently laid Damien down, removed their hats, and stood there waiting for further instructions. As Vivian turned towards the bed with her mixture in hand, both men covered their noses and mouths with their hats. The smell of the concoction was intense and almost took their breath away. Vivian waved the mixture under Damien's nose, and after a few seconds, which seemed to move more like an hour, Damien's chest rose, and an unconscious cough came from him. Vivian moved the concoction from his nose, placed a cork in the vial, and smiled while she touched his face.

Vivan said, "I knew you were still in there."

The two men were standing there in astonishment, and Hassan said, "You're not a healer; you are a miracle worker."

Vivian smiled at him and said, "Thank you both for all you have done. I need to get him cleaned up now and work on his wounds."

Hassan replied, "What else can we do to help?"

Vivian touched both of their hands and said, "You have done enough getting him here. I am in your debt."

Hassan smiled at her, looked at Yusuf, and motioned towards the door. Both the men smiled and walked out the door, closing it behind them.

Chapter 3

Deep in the entrails of existence lies the Seven Realms of Hell, each a layer of an infernal puzzle crafted by the Sovereign of Shadows. Each layer reveals a fragment of the Soverign's darkness and is carved from the essence of torment, temptation, and despair. These layers are not just the realms of punishment but living extensions of the Sovereign's dominion. The layers are interconnected by the Sovereign's boundless power, and through them, the Sovereign exerts its influence on mortal and immortal souls alike, all the while tightening his grasp on all that exists in shadow. In the center of it all, the Sovereign exists from the energy of the tormented, its eyes ever-watchful, its will ever-commanding. The Sovereign reigns over all the dominion of Hell.

The Sovereign of Shadows commands its messenger, Humilis, to inform the generals they would come to meet the next day to give their reports. If the plan was not progressing, some new generals may be found. The Sovereign knew that if the timing was missed on the plan, it would take another century before it could be attempted again. The messenger bowed his head slowly, backed out of the Sovereign's sight, and took flight for all the layers of hell.

The messenger arrived at the First Layer, Terischa – The Realm of Whispers. This swirling, eternal fog cloaks the endless expanse, muting all sound except for the insidious whispers that seem to originate from nowhere and everywhere at once. The terrain is treacherous, an unruly mix of jagged rocks, shallow pools of dark, reflective water, and shifting ground that never stabilizes. A faint flicker of ghostly light in the mist disorients and deceives, leading travelers deeper into despair. The fog is alive, curling and coiling around the damned, cold and wet like the touch of a corpse, seeping into their lungs with each panicked breath.

Zephyion, the Shadowblade, commands this spectral nightmare. He stands eight feet tall and wide and is cloaked in armor that keeps his true form hidden from view and seems to dissolve into the mist. His deputy, Nyxis the Echo, ensures the whispers carry the sharpest edge of torment. Nyxis manifests as a formless voice that mimics the fears, regrets, and self-loathing of the souls trapped within Terischa. She guides them into illusions of salvation, only to watch them plunge deeper into despair when their hopes crumble.

This layer is the domain of the hesitant, those who were betrayers, and those who allowed their vacillation or whispered lies to destroy others. Politicians who misled nations, friends who sowed gossip that fractured lives, and lovers who whispered promises they never intended to honor. They are the ones that continuously wander about this fog, eternally lost. Their ears bled from the unceasing whispers of their own deceit, and the pools reflect not their faces but the broken lives they left behind.

Humilis approached Zephyion and said, "The Sovereign commands your presence tomorrow night for your report on your progress on its plan."

Zephyion looked down upon the puny messenger and growled his reply, "I will be there to report on my great progress." Then, he kicks the messenger away from him.

Humilis twisted across the ground and caught flight after something hard stopped him. He took flight dizzily and landed in the second layer, Nashcatri – The Smoldering Eden. Nashcatri is a place of cruel, otherworldly beauty. The forests of glowing plants emit lights the color of various gemstones so radiant that it blinds as much as it illuminates. The air is thick with intoxicating scents that lure even the most wary. Rivers of molten gold flow between the foliage with heat scalding yet oddly mesmerizing. The skies are a kaleidoscope of swirling colors, beautiful but suffocating, pressing down upon someone like a velvet weight. The various genera of flowers hum with an eerie, pulsing sound that captivates the mind into taking a closer look at them. Their petals tremble like nervous, fleshy appendages eager to ensnare.

The messenger approached Lilith, the Bloodthirsty, whose command over Nashcatri was done from her crimson throne and surrounded by her Infernal Vanguards. Lilith the Blood-thirsty is a deadly paradox of seduction and terror, her flawless beauty concealing the monstrous predator beneath. With her long, luscious obsidian hair and enchanting, burning ruby eyes, she lures souls into the depths of desire, twisting their cravings into eternal torment. Her voice, a melody of honeyed venom, ensnares even the strongest wills, while her crimson lips and cruel smile promise ecstasy laced with agony. Clad in a shadowy gown that flickered like glowing embers, she radiated an aura of both allure and menace. When her true form emerged, her elegance transformed into a fiery nightmare with jagged talons, a gaping maw, and the tortured wail of consumed souls, which marked her as the ultimate predator. Both ruler and reflection of Nashcatri's horrors, Lilith's beauty is a trap whose cruelty guaranteed no escape.

Lilith's trusted second-in-command, Thaldris the Ensnarer, took pleasure in the creation of intricate traps that forced souls to confront their deepest desires. Thaldris appeared as a celestial being of impossible beauty. His weaved illusions made the damned believe they were on the brink of fulfilling their deepest desires. But every time they had reached their prize, it turned to molten agony, feeding Lilith's unending hunger for control.

The damned in Nashcatri are those that have been consumed by their own desires. The unfaithful lovers, the greedy, the thieves, the power-hungry leaders, and all who have crushed others in their pursuits. These souls wandered endlessly, drawn to illusions of their deepest cravings: a loved one's embrace, unearned riches, or a crown of sovereignty. All that was only for their prizes to twist into monstrous, fiery forms that consumed them. Their screams echoed in the golden rivers, which fed the Sovereign's hunger for mortal despair.

Once the messenger of the Sovereign stepped in front of Lilith, he said, "The Sovereign summoned you to meet with all the generals tomorrow to discuss the plan."

Lilith's ruby eyes flicked toward Humilis with a look of cold contempt that might have frozen lesser souls in place. She offered no words, only a faint, dismissive nod. Thaldris took this silent cue as all the permission needed. With a smirk, he seized the trembling creature by its scrawny neck with his clawed fingers pressing deep enough to draw wisps of black ichor and hurled him skyward with brutal force. The messenger flailed into the air, but his innate resilience took over. His wings unfurled as he twisted his trajectory into a steady, reluctant flight. Despite the humiliation burning in his chest, he pressed onward toward the frozen wasteland of the third layer. The Sovereign's will could not be denied, even if it meant enduring endless abuse.

The Sovereign's messenger entered the third Layer of Hell. Salicuthie – The Frozen Abyss, a barren tundra that stretched endlessly in all directions. An unexpected climate not discussed or known by anyone outside the realms of Hell. Its white expanse was only broken by jagged ice spires that reached like the grasping hands of the damned. The air was so cold it burned; each breath sliced through a being's lungs like frozen daggers. Beneath the ice, shadowed memories of failure and regret shifted and writhed, frozen in their eternal torment. Each step cracked the brittle surface, revealing glimpses of agonized faces trapped just beneath, their frozen mouths still mouthed cries for release.

Morgath the Dreadbringer presides over this desolate frozen wasteland. Morgath's twisted skeletal form was cloaked in frost and shadow. His form was that of a large humanoid with the skeletal head of a caribou. His massive form towered over humans and most demons alike. His second-in-command, Iskren the Witherer, a dark wraith, moved silently over the ice like the cold wind. He froze not only flesh but the very will of those he touched. Iskren whispered lies of false hope to the frozen, tricking them into the belief that escape was possible, only to shatter their spirits when their efforts failed.

Salicuthie was reserved for those who abandoned others in their time of need: parents who turned away from their children, leaders who abandoned their people, and friends who left others to perish. These souls are encased in ice, their bodies rigid, their minds reliving their failures on endless loops. As the cold seeped into them, they lost more and more of their identity until only their regrets remained.

Humilis made his way through the cold wind of Salicuthie, not daring to stop, for he knew if he stopped, he would be frozen. After he fought through the winds and made it to Morgath's presence, he heard in his mind, "What does the Sovereign command now?"

Humilis thought, "The Sovereign commands your presence with all the generals tomorrow to discuss the plan."

Morgath mentally relayed to him, "I will be there. Be gone before Iskren's touch is the last thing you feel."

Humilis saw Iskren moving towards him with his icy fingers outstretched. With that deadly thought in his mind, the messenger turned and stretched his wings. The cold wind caught his wings, lifted him out of Iskren's reach, and pushed him over the frozen landscape of Salicuthie. The cold winds that seemed to freeze his hot blood never felt so welcomed. The Sovereign's messenger moved on towards the fourth layer of Hell, Resxlun.

Humilis whispered, "One day, the Sovereign will see the dedication and boundless length I go and promote me to a more fitting position for my devotion to it."

Upon his arrival in Rsxulun, The clockwork Maze Humilis winced at the sound of grinding, a ceaseless cacophony of gears that filled the air. He looked out upon the labyrinth of colossal metal contraptions and endless pathways as they shifted. The walls, floors, and ceilings are all part of the ever-moving mechanism that gleamed with a slick, oily sheen that seemed almost alive. Sparks flew as gears locked and unlocked, which created a blind, unpredictable light that disoriented those who wandered within. Sometimes, the gears dripped blood while the sound of bones and flesh ground between them, which produced the sound of faint screams, as if the maze itself was alive and fed on the tormented.

Here, Kuloth the Malevolent holds dominion, seated tall above the chaos on his mechanized throne. Kuloth the Malevolent is a looming nightmare of flesh and machinery, his body a grotesque fusion of crude metal and translucent skin through which gears and pistons churn infinitely. His glowing, orange-yellow eyes burn white-hot within darkened sockets of bone and flesh. His grotesque mechanical maw was lined with milling, bloodstained teeth. He is shrouded in a tattered cloak of black steel fibers that flicker with ember-like light, with only the lower half of his body covered with a black-on-black kilt. Kuloth fully embodied the maze's cruel precision, unfeeling, calculating, and mercilessness.

His Chief Engineer of Torment, Threxil the Tinkerer, devises traps and mechanisms that alter the maze at a whim. Threxil's creations include mechanical beasts that stalk the corridors, feeding on the fear of the damned. He took particular delight in giving false paths that lead to nowhere but the crushing grip of gears. Threxil delighted in the sound of the crushing bones, ripped flesh, and screams of agony of those tormented in Rsxulun.

This layer of Hell entrapped the cunning manipulators, those who used lies and deceit to weave webs of suffering. Lawyers who twisted the truth, criminals who built empires on lies, and tyrants who ruled through propaganda are condemned here. Those who manipulated others and stole time from those who trusted and relied on them. They are forced to navigate the maze, only to have their paths cut short by grinding gears that slice through flesh and bone.

Upon Humilis' arrival, the machinery alerted Kuloth and Threxil to his presence. The machinery moved to open a path direct to Kuloth, not out of respect, but to ensure Humilis' presence lasted as short as possible.

Humilis looked upon Kuloth and said, "The Sovereign commands your presence tomorrow to discuss the plan with all the other generals."

Kuloth looked upon him with contempt and, without a word of acknowledgment, grabbed Humilis and threw him back the way he came. Humilis could only hope for Kuloth's sake that this was an acknowledgment of the message. He took control of the trajectory and began on his way to Rahul.

Upon Humilis' arrival in the fifth layer of Hell, the overwhelming stench of rot filled his nostrils. Rahul, The City of Endless Hunger, was a metropolis of grotesque decay, where the streets were lined with piles of rotting, pulsating food. Buildings were crafted from warped, organic materials, with walls that breathed and roofs that drank rotten liquid, which created an overwhelming sense of suffocation. Along with the thick, putrid stench, the cries of ravenous souls echoed endlessly through the streets. Food was served on banquet tables that stretched endlessly, the fare glistening with sickly fluids. The more the damned eat, the hungrier they become, their stomachs stretched grotesquely before they split open, only to heal and start again.

Azrzel the Infernal was a fiery and imposing ruler who oversaw their dominion from a grand palace made of sinew and bone. Their form was that of a grand hostess dressed for a fabulous ball. Azrzel's gown was made of the finest fruits in all the universe, which created an even more imposing presence to the gluttonous. Azrzel's beauty and charisma enchanted everyone except their fellow demons who stood in their presence.

Their second-in-command, Vorath the Glutton, oversaw the grotesque banquets where souls were forced to eat endlessly, only to find their hunger deepened with every bite. Vorath's form shifted constantly between a beautiful temptress and a handsome seducer who would encourage the lost souls to enjoy the suffrage. They embodied the torment of insatiable greed. They ensured every morsel eaten fed not the damned but the Sovereign's insidious power.

Rahul claimed those who succumbed to greed in life: gluttons who hoarded food while others starved, moguls who exploited the weak for profit, and those who amassed wealth with no regard for charity. Here, they are cursed with an unquenchable hunger to feast on that which provided no sustenance. Their bodies grew monstrous and grotesque as they gorged, only to decay and reform. Rahul ensured that their torment never ended.

Humilis flew to Azrzel's presence and passed on the message from the Sovereign. Azrzel gave him an enchanted smile and they nodded in acknowledgment. Humilis awaited his abuse and forced departure, but Azrzel just looked upon him as they waited to hear more. Then Vorath pointed Humilis toward the table of rotted food and beckoned him to partake. With that, Humilis hastened his retreat from their presence and began his journey to Lebun.

As Humilis entered the Sixth Layer of Hell he shuddered as

he knew it lived up to its name even for him. Lebun, The Pit of Mockery, a grand coliseum of endless humiliation. The stands were filled with faceless wraiths whose jeers reverberated like thunder as every soul was forced to relive their most significant failures and mocked. The ground was cracked and scorched, and the air was alive with the energy of derision and despair. Massive mirrors lined the walls, showing twisted reflections of those within that amplified their shame. Their faces distorted grotesquely in the glass and exaggerated every flaw and failure until they became monstrous parodies of their former selves.

Anthrax the Undying was a hulking oversized human male with the head of a skeletal bull. He oversaw this realm with pure evil and cruelty. Anyone who gets out of line with him feels the hash and painful swing of his flail. This massive spiked flail swung on chains rusted from the blood it had torn through over the years. This weapon was forged upon the fires of the humiliated and wails like the tormented when it is swung.

His herald, Calyx the Jester, was a complete converse to the general. She dances between the damned, mimicking their failures with exaggerated, grotesque performances. Calyx's laughter is infectious and warped even the souls themselves into unwilling participants of their own humiliation. She twisted their memories, making them believe their past glories were always failures. Nothing of the tormented was left as a happy memory.

Lebun ensnared the prideful ones. Those who lorded their achievements over others, humiliated rivals, or built their lives on arrogance. They were forced to watch as their grandest moments turned into farcical failures, each replayed endlessly before the faceless crowd. Their pride rotted into despair, and they became part of the jeering audience, mocking others in a desperate attempt to escape their own torment.

Humilis went directly to Anthrax and delivered the Sovereign's message. Anthrax looked down upon Humilis and gave him a nod that signified he understood. As Humilis turned to leave Calyx cartwheeled in front of him, smiled, and jesterd toward the crowd with an invitation to join the tormented. Humilis declined and flew off as fast as he could and left this layer behind and proceeded to Westerflau, his final stop.

Humilis approached the Seventh Layer of Hell. Wasterflau, The Void Beyond Reason, was the most profound and most chaotic realm. The Void, as most called it, was a place where reality dissolved into swirling colors and maddening sounds. There was no ground and only a sense that one floated in a vast, windless, and ever-shifting vacant space. The rules of existence were rewritten at the whim of who oversaw this layer. Gravity fluctuated, time looped, and the very fabric of perception tore, leaving souls to dissolve into formlessness. The air hummed with discordant tones that burrowed into the mind, which unraveled thoughts and memories until not one spark of coherence remained.

At the heart of this chaos, Noctherion the Blackvein resided, a spectral shadow that whirled like a ghostly fog with pulsating veins of dark blue light. He was the Sovereign's inquisitor and could extract information from the most hardened of creatures. Just a scratch from his clawed hands could poison a being without a known antidote.

His second-in-command, Vorex the Nullifier, wielded the power to unmake thoughts and memories He ensured no soul could retain any sense of self making their mind weak and vulnerable. Vorex's presence reduced even the strongest mind to gibbering fragments, their essence fed directly into the Sovereign's limitless will which enhanced his power.

Wasterflau was reserved for the maddest of beings. The most criminally insane, serial killers, torturers, and heretics. All those who defied the natural order defiled those they crossed, preached lies, or spread chaos for their own gain. Here, their minds unravel entirely, each fragment of thought spinning off into the void to form new torments. Everything they did in the past is done to them and increased in disparity. They float endlessly, unable to distinguish themselves from the chaos around them until they become indistinguishable from the Void itself and a part of the Sovereign's infinite power.

Humilis announced himself unto the void and waited for Noctherion to acknowledge him. He knew better than to cross into that domain.

Noctherion appeared and said, "What does the master command of me?"

Humilis replied, "He called for all his generals tomorrow to discuss the plan."

Noctherion said, "I will do as he commands." Then, it dissolved back into the void.

Humilis flew back to the Sovereign and told him all the generals acknowledged that they would be at the meeting. The Sovereign nodded at him and waved its hand, signaling Humilis was dismissed.

Chapter 4

Sitting on the bed's edge, the demon inside still fought Damien. His words still lingered on his lips as he got up to join Vivian for a meal at the table. In his heart, he knew that it could be good to tell her, yet it could end badly. It would be a new start in their lives either way, and he knew she reciprocated the same feelings he had. Damien knew that if he did not tell her, he could lose her, but also, if he told her, he would lose her in the future. "Such a coward," boomed the voice in his head.

Damien looked around and expected to see someone this time, then thought, "A coward I am not and I just need time to work it out."

Azrathis responded, "Tell her your feelings, and I will find a way to ensure she lives through the cursed childbirth."

Damien chuckled, "And what would that cost me."

Azrathis said, "The cost would be my freedom. My freedom from you for the life of your beloved."

Vivian stepped back into the room and sat a warm meal of

venison stew and fresh barms.

After she had placed the meal on the table, she began to serve it up in two bowls. Damien sat and looked at her with longing. It was not until Vivian turned and smiled at him that he realized he was staring at her. The whole of his body had a warm sensation from her look, as though the sun had broken through the clouds and shone upon him. "Do you plan to just stare or are you ready to eat?" Vivian said.

Damion returned with, "I am hungry now, and I will stare while I eat."

Vivian giggled. "That won't be awkward at all while we dine, and incidentally, you will walk in here under your own power."

Damien stood up more slowly, saying, "I will make my way now."

Damien was carefully rising off of the bed edge onto his feet as his boots softly creaked on the hardwood flooring.

Every step towards the table felt heavier, the weight of his unconfessed confession upon his chest like an iron chain binding him. However, when his eyes sought out Vivian again, a quiet strength stirred inside him. She was radiant, even in the most unspectacular moments in the way her auburn hair caught the firelight, in the way her hands dealt out the meal as if the act in and of itself was some sort of art. He reached the table and sat opposite her, his fingers brushing the carved edge of the chair as if he anchored himself to this moment. Vivian slid a bowl of stew in front of him and treated him to that smile that felt like a blow to his heart.

"You know," Vivian said lightly, breaking the silence as she folded her hands in her lap. "You've been acting strange lately. More brooding than usual, and that's saying something."

Damien chuckled low in his throat, though his voice came out strained as a bowstring pulled too tight. "Brooding is a skill I've honed over the years. I didn't think you'd notice an increase."

"Oh, I notice everything, Damien," she said, cocking her head slightly, her bright green eyes fastening onto his with an inquisitive intensity. "You've had something on your mind for days now, haven't you?

The question between them was as sharp as an arrow, caught without ambiguity. Damien clutched onto the table edge until the flesh whitened into his knuckles. Deep down, Azrathis moved without sound; its voice behind his mind-vein became soft and serpentine.

Say it, little man. Barely reveal your soul or let the very silence condemn her to a fate too terrible for words.

Slowly, Damien exhaled as he clamped his jaw shut. He inched forward on the couch, setting his elbows on the table as his eyes met Vivian's. "Vivian," he started off in a low, husky tone, "something's been weighing on me. Something I should have told you a while back.

Vivian's spoon halted in mid-air as her expression softened and she set it back down, her body angling forward to match his. A flicker of concern danced in the emerald eyes. "What is it, Damien?" she asked in a quiet tone, her voice steady even though her face betrayed her worry.

Damien's throat was dry, the words clawing at him from within. He had fought beasts and men, but this, this was something far more terrifying. He could feel his pulse hammering in his ears as he forced himself to continue.

"I've always tried to protect you," Damien said finally, his voice shaking but firm. "To shield you from the darkness in my life, from the things I've done. and the things I am. But in doing that, I've hidden a part of myself that I can't keep from you anymore.

Vivian's eyebrows furrowed, and a faint crease appeared between them as she searched his face. "Damien," she said gently, "what are you trying to say?

He held her gaze, his now fierce and unyielding, the storm in his soul breaking free. "I love you, Vivian. I have loved you from the moment we met, and I have been a fool to keep it to myself. I thought. I thought I was sparing you. Sparing you from me, from the curse I carry. But the truth is, I cannot imagine a life without you. I do not want a life without you."

Vivian's lips parted as her breath stopped in her throat. Thereafter, for what seemed a small eternity, neither of them moved, the crackling fire the only sound in the room.

"And." Damien finished, his voice even now, but his heart racing in his chest like a jackrabbit, "I want to marry you. Not because I'm trying to defy fate or outwit this curse, but because you're the only thing in this world that makes life worth living. If you'll have me. if you'll take the risk. I'll spend the rest of my life proving to you that I am worthy of your love."

Vivian's hand reached across the table, her slim fingers curling around his big, rough calloused hand as it trembled slightly. Her fingers wrapped tight around his in a warm hold.

"Damien," she whispered, her voice husky with emotion. Her eyes shone bright with unshed tears as she smiled, the corners of her mouth quivering. "You've always been so stubborn. Did you think I didn't already know? That I couldn't see it in every glance, every word, and every time you stood between me and harm?"

He blinked in shock. "You knew?"

Vivian let out a small, throaty laugh and shook her head. "Of course I knew, but hearing from your lips. Damien, it has taken long enough. Yes, I'll marry you. Curse or no curse, I simply don't care. Whatever comes, we'll face it together.".

The room seemed to grow warmer, as if the fire itself had responded to her words. Damien squeezed her hand tightly, his heart swelling with a mixture of relief and joy so profound it almost brought him to his knees. He opened his mouth to speak again, but the voice of Xandros slithered through his thoughts, coiling around his newfound happiness like smoke.

"Foolish, brave, but foolish. Now, mortal, let us see how far you're willing to go to keep that promise."

Damien pushed the voice aside, his gaze fixed on Vivian. In her eyes, he saw everything he'd fought for and everything he was willing to fight for again. "Together," he echoed softly, and for the first time in years, hope bloomed in his chest.

The warmth of that moment still fluttered between them, a fragile golden thing that was, in some incredible way, refusing shadows that seemed to draw closer outside. Damien held Vivian's eyes, his hand still clasped tightly in hers, when an anguished and frantic pounding echoed from outside the door, the sudden sound shattering the silence, booming like thunder in this little room. Both moved sharply toward the door as one voice called, strained with urgent appeal.

Chapter 5

The quiet room, heavy with the budding warmth between Damien and Vivian, reverberated with the Rabbi's fist against the door as if it were thunder. Both of them turned sharply, instantly snapping their gazes toward the door as his desperate voice cut through the night.

"Damien! Vivian! Open up!" he shouted, his voice hoarse and out of breath. "Another child has gone missing, just hours ago! We need your help now!"

In an instant, Damien was on his feet, his body taut with purpose. His hand instinctively went to the hilt of his sword, its familiar weight grounding him as his dark eyes met Vivian's. "I must help," he said, his voice low but unwavering, a quiet declaration meant as much for her as it was for the demon that stirred restlessly within him.

Vivian stood as well, her expression resolute despite the flicker of worry in her emerald eyes. "Then I'm coming with you," she said firmly, her voice leaving no room for debate.

"No." Damien stepped closer to her, his hands settling on

her shoulders. His touch was both protective and pleading, his voice soft but unyielding. "If this is what I think it is, if the curse has spread, I need you safe. You've seen what this darkness can do."

Vivian's jaw clenched as she met his gaze. "And I've seen what you can't do alone. I'm coming with you, Damien, and there's nothing you can say to stop me."

Before he could get another protest out, Azrathis slithered into his thoughts, its voice curling like smoke through his mind.

"Ah, the brave little bird. It doesn't dawn on her you are the storm she is flying into, does it? Let her come, mortal. Let her see the full weight of your burden. Or better yet. let her be the anchor that drags you both to ruin."

He clenched his jaw, and forced the voice back into the recesses of his mind. He turned toward the Rabbi, who stood framed in the doorway, his breath misting in the cold night air, his face pale with dread. "Where was the child last seen?" Damien asked, his tone clipped, urgent.

The Rabbi wrung his hands together, twisting the fabric of his robe. "Near the woods, by the old well," he said in a shaking tone. "But before you take off like lightning, you have to talk to the girl's family. They will tell you all they can and they must understand that something has taken the child. The people in the entire village are terror-stricken."

Damien nodded, turning back to Vivian. His gaze was dark and heavy. "Fine," he said, quieter now, almost resigned. "But if you're coming, you stay close to me. No running off, no heroics. Promise me that."

Vivian crossed her arms, her chin lifting slightly. "I promise," she said, though the fire in her eyes left little doubt that she would do whatever was necessary.

The three stepped out into the night: the cold bit at their faces while the village lay in an uncomfortable silence; the lanterns barely glowing, swung in the wind, sending jittery shadows to crawl along the edges of buildings. The Rabbi took them in quick strides, his robe fluttering, hurrying to the outskirts of the village.

"This way," he said tightly. "Her family's house is just ahead."

The cottage they approached was small and unassuming, its thatched roof shining with frost in the pale moonlight. The door was open slightly, faint sobs muffled and escaping into the night. The Rabbi hesitated at the threshold, his face somber as he turned to them.

"They're inside," he whispered. "Go easy with them. They are barely hanging on.".

Damien stepped forward and, with a light tap on the door-frame, pushed it open. What lay inside was a heart-shattering scene: there she sat at the rough wooden table, her face hidden in her hands, the shoulders shaking hard, hard with silent sobs, and next to her, he walked up and down, his fingers pulling at his hair, wide, bloodshot eyes full of fear.

"Who—who's there?" the man asked, his voice cracking as he turned toward them.

"The Rabbi sent us," Damien said, stepping fully into the room. His deep, steady voice filled the space, his commanding presence immediately drawing their attention. "We're here to help. Tell us what happened."

The man, stunned, stopped his pacing; hands fell limply to his sides as his eyes darted from Damien to Vivian. His wife slowly raised her tear-streaked face, her pale, trembling hands clutching a piece of cloth as though it were a lifeline.

"Our daughter… Eliza," she began, her voice low and barely

audible. "She... she went to the woods this afternoon to gather berries and kindling. She wanted to help me make a pie for her father." Her voice cracked, and fresh tears spilled down her cheeks as she buried her face in her hands once more.

The man laid a shaking hand on her shoulder as he continued, his voice tight with emotion. "She was supposed to come back before dark," he said, the words tumbling out in a rush. "She's always good about that and always came straight back. But when the sun set and she still wasn't home, I went looking for her. I found her basket near the old well, just lying there. No sign of her. Nothing."

Vivian came closer, her voice soft yet firm. "How old is she? And in which part of the woods did she usually go?

She's seven, the mother whispered, her knuckles white as she clutched the cloth in her lap. And she usually stays close to the path near the well. She knows not to go far, but... but the shadows have been strange lately. People have been whispering about the woods being cursed again.

The father's voice was suddenly sharp, desperation surfacing in every word. "Please, you have to find her. She's just a little girl. She couldn't have gone far. Something took her, I know it."

Damien stepped closer, his tone resolute. "We will find her," he said firmly. His dark gaze shifted to Vivian, their eyes locking in shared determination. "We'll start at the well and work outward. If she's anywhere near, we'll find her."

Vivian nodded, her own voice steady. "We won't let her stay out there a moment longer than she has to."

The mother's sobs softened as she looked at them, wide, tear-filled eyes pleading. "Thank you," she said in a small voice. "Please... please bring her back to us."

As they emerged out under the icy night from the cottage into the cold, he could feel Azrathis stirred once more, the voice slithering through his thoughts like a shadow curled around his resolution.

"Ah, such noble intentions, mortal. But tell me, what will you do when you find what's waiting for you in those woods? What if it's more than shadows this time? Will you still have the courage to be her savior… or will you crumble when she sees the darkness you carry?"

Damien gritted his teeth, forcing the voice into silence as he tightened his grip on the hilt of his sword. Beside him, Vivian placed a hand on his arm, her touch grounding him in the present.

"We'll find her, Damien," she said firmly, her voice cutting through the night's chill. "Whatever's out there, we'll face it together."

He nodded, the weight of the task settling heavily on his shoulders as they approached the edge of the woods. The faint glow of the lanterns faded behind them, leaving only the thick, restless darkness ahead. The forest loomed, its towering trees twisting into the night sky, their shadows breathing with an almost sentient malice. Damien steeled himself and stepped forward; the darkness closed in around them like a living thing.

Cold, oppressive darkness seemed to cling to Damien and Vivian as they entered the forest. Leaves rustled lightly as if sharing secrets, one tree with another. The night itself almost breathed an air thick with tension. Damien knew this weight stirring inside his mind, the demon slowly emerging.

In a low voice, evil dripping from each word, it slipped out of its cage, "Brave steps, mortal, but tell me, will you save the girl, or at last, will the shadows claim you? I'll be watching."

Chapter 6

The woods swallowed them whole.   Every step swallowed Damien and Vivian deeper into someplace of twisting shadows and whispering trees. Heavy, the air was thick with damp earth and decaying leaves; the faint moonlight hardly broke through the canopy above. Narrowed, the path to the old well was choked by brambles and gnarled roots that reached for their boots like grasping hands.

Damien forged ahead, his sword at the ready, his senses on high alert. The cold, unforgiving steel was a comfort in his hand, though he knew it might be little use against what awaited them. Behind him, Vivian clutched a lantern, its flickering light casting uneasy shadows that danced across the skeletal branches.

"This place feels…..wrong," Vivian whispered, barely loud enough to be heard.

He nodded somberly. "The woods have always been strange at night, but this," He paused, his head cocking a trifle as if he was listening. "This is different."

They approached the old well. The crumbling stones were

slick with moss and frost. Damien squatted beside its edge, his eyes scanning the surrounding ground with practiced precision. "This must be where the girl dropped her basket," he said in that low, measured voice. He pointed to a patch of disturbed earth. "Footprints. She was here."

Vivian knelt beside him, the beam of her lantern casting a faint glow over the area. "But look here," she said, her voice tight. "These prints are larger, heavier, and they overlap hers. Someone or something followed her."

Damien traced the prints with his gloved hand, his brow furrowing. The larger tracks were strange, too long, with claw-like impressions at the tips. They weren't human. "This isn't an animal I've ever seen," he muttered. "These tracks, whatever made them, weren't meant to walk this earth."

Vivian's breath caught. "Damien, look." She nodded toward the bottom of the well. A fragment of material caught on a jutting stone, its edges torn and frayed. "That must be from her dress."

Damien carefully took the cloth in his hand and examined it. It was damp and emitted a faint scent of sulfur, and his stomach roiled. "This isn't normal," he said, his voice tight with unease. "There's something else here."

A soft wind rustled through the trees, and upon it was a soft, unearthly sound—a faraway and distorted child's laugh. The two of them went quite still, heads jerking to scan the shadows.

"Did you hear that?" Vivian asked, fingers tightening on the lantern.

Damien nodded, and his body tensed as his free hand floated near the hilt of his sword. "It's not her," he said with firm conviction. "That is not a sound any living child would make."

Azrathis stirred suddenly in him, curling into his thoughts

like smoke.

"You're blundering in the dark, mortal," it hissed, mocking yet seductive. "Let me give you a taste of what I can offer. A gift, if you will. Perhaps then you'll understand why you need me."

The weird feeling washed over him before Damien could answer. It was as though the darkness around him shifted, its smothering veil pulled back. The shadows were no longer impenetrable; he could see. Every tree, every twisted root, every gnarled branch became clear to his eyes as though bathed in silver light. He could even make out faint, glowing trails where the strange footprints led deeper into the woods.

Damien let out a sharp intake of breath, his hand tightening around his sword. "What have you done?" he thought, his mental voice a growl.

"Consider it a small demonstration," Azrathis purred, satisfaction oozing into every word. "Your mortal eyes are so limited. This is but the beginning of what I can offer. Use it wisely, mortal. But be careful not to let her see you moving too surely, or she'll start to wonder what you've become."

Damien's jaw tightened. He forced his expression to remain neutral as he turned to Vivian. "Stay close," he said, his voice steady. "We'll follow the tracks."

He raised a hand as if to shield his eyes from the dim light of the lantern, an unnecessary act now that his vision pierced the darkness. He didn't douse the lantern; he couldn't let Vivian suspect, but his mind reeled at this unwanted gift. The woods looked different now, more alive yet more sinister. Shadows slithered in the corners of his vision, unnatural and watchful.

"Damien," Vivian said, breaking into his reverie. "There's something over there." She pointed toward the underbrush, where a faint glimmer caught the light of the lantern.

Damien stepped forward cautiously. His enhanced sight homed in immediately on the thing there. It was a child's doll, its face cracked and smeared with dirt. The fabric dress was damp and hung a faint, sulfurous scent in the air.

Vivian knelt beside him, her voice shaking. "That's hers. I've seen her carrying it around the village."

Damien's stomach roiled, but he made himself focus. "The footprints go deeper," he said, nodding toward the faint trail lit by his new sight. "But they're getting more erratic, less like walking, more like dragging."

Vivian's face went white. "Damien. If this is what I think it is……"

"I know," he said shortly, cutting her off. He turned back to her, his face impassive. "This isn't something we can handle alone. We have to go back. We'll need a search party, people who know the woods, and dogs to track her scent."

Vivian hesitated but nodded, holding the doll tightly. "If she's still alive, we need to hurry. Whatever took her-"

"-isn't waiting," Damien finished, his voice grim.

On their way back, Damien picked up more signs: a broken branch here, scratch marks gouged into the bark of a tree there. The whispers of the forest grew louder and more insistent, a chorus of unseen voices that seemed to implore him to turn back.

When they finally emerged from the woods into the village, the faint light of the lanterns in the square was almost blinding after the suffocating darkness of the forest. People were gathered in the square, their faces pale with fear, as whispers spread through the crowd.

"We need a search party," Damien announced, his deep voice

cutting through the murmurs. "Gather your strongest men, the best hounds you have. The trail leads into the woods, but what we're dealing with isn't natural."

"What do you mean?" one of the men asked, his voice shaking.

Damien hesitated, his eyes scanning across the frightened villagers. "There is evidence of something dark," he finally said, "something powerful. If we are going to save that girl, now would be the time to act."

The Rabbi, near the front of the mob, pushed forward. "What more is to be done?" his voice squeaked. "The men and the dogs will be mobilized, but if this darkness is what I fear, what more shall aid?"

Damien turned to him, his face grim. "Get the community to pray," he ordered his voice firm. "Now. Get them to congregate in the temple, light candles, and pray for her soul. If she has been taken where I believe she has, prayers may be the only thing that will slow down her descent. It may buy us time.

The Rabbi's face paled further, but he nodded. "I'll see to it immediately." He turned to a group of women standing nearby. "Go to the temple and tell everyone to come, and begin the prayers. Don't stop until I return."

As the women hurried away, Vivian looked at Damien, her face troubled. "Do you really think it'll work?" she asked softly.

His eyes darted to the woods, his jaw setting tight. "I don't know," he finally admitted. "But if it may just be able to, then we must give it a try. We fight for her here, and they'll fight for her soul there."

Azrathis stirred again, his voice sliding into Damien's mind like a dagger.

"How touching. Do you really think your prayers can stop what's already in motion? She's already slipping closer to me.

Will you truly make it in time, or will you arrive only to see her consumed by the very darkness you fear?"

Damien gritted his teeth and turned back toward the woods, ignoring the voice. "We don't have time to waste," he said. "Get the search party ready as soon as possible. The darkness is stirring, and they aren't waiting on us."

The woods had given up their secrets grudgingly. As Damien and Vivian emerged from the smothering darkness, the weight of what they'd seen clung to the chill night air. The village square churned with fidgeting murmurs, lanterns casting wild flickers on every face. The men grasped makeshift arms. Axes, pitchforks, anything at all while the rest heaved ropes and baskets to carry whatever could be found in stores. Tension was alive in palpable folds of fear, rolling through the crowd like a life form.

"We'll need the dogs," Damien said, his voice cutting through the murmurs. "Bring them here now, and something the girl has touched, her scent is all we'll have to guide us in the dark."

One of them nodded and disappeared into the crowd, returning momentarily with two powerful hounds tugging on their leashes. Their handlers were fighting to restrain them, barking and whining as if picking up on the unease in the air.

Vivian stepped forward, holding out the doll they'd found near the well. "This is hers," she said, her voice steady though her hands shook. "Let them smell it.

The dogs were brought closer, their wet noses snuffling frantically at the fissured and muddied doll. One growled low within its throat and yelped out a bright, urgent bark. The other bucked hard into his leash and nearly pulled the handler off into the woods.

"They've got the scent," Damien said, with an edge. "We move now."

He turned to the men who had gathered, his dark eyes scanning their anxious faces. "Stay close. Keep your lanterns and torches lit no matter what. The woods are different tonight. They're alive with something dark, and it's watching us. Whatever happens, do not wander off alone. If you hear something, call out. Do not go after it on your own."

The men nodded, pale-faced and some shaking their hands on their weapons.

"Rabbi," Damien turned to the older man who stood near the temple steps, "You know what to do."

The Rabbi inclined his head solemnly. "We will gather everyone in the temple and begin the prayers. We won't stop until you return."

"Good," Damien replied, his tone firm but distracted. His attention was already shifting to the dark line of trees at the edge of the village, their twisted shapes swaying ominously in the wind. "Pray hard. It might be the only thing keeping her from slipping beyond our reach."

Vivian stepped up beside him, her hand brushing his arm briefly. "We're ready," she said softly.

Damien gave her a curt nod and turned back to the villagers. "Let's move," he ordered, his voice carrying over the crackle of torches and the low growls of the dogs.

The search party began its trek into the woods, lanterns and torches bobbing in the darkness like fireflies. The hounds led the way, their noses to the ground, pulling their handlers forward. Damien kept himself near the head, his sword out, his enhanced sight serving him well. Though he still carried a lantern, he kept its dim light swinging to one side, his careful not to reveal how clear he could see through the ink shadows.

Vivian walked beside him, her own lantern casting a soft, steady glow. Her free hand gripped the strap of a small satchel she'd brought along, filled with herbs and charms meant to ward off evil. She hadn't said much since they'd set out, her jaw tight and her focus unwavering.

The deeper they walked, the more the forest closed in around them. The air grew colder, and the trees huddled closer together as if conspiring to keep them out or trap them within. Gone was the faint wind that whispered through the village; instead, an eerie stillness made every snap of a twig beneath their boots echo like a thunderclap.

The dogs stopped suddenly, their hackles rising as they growled low in their throats. The lead handler leaned down, whispering softly to calm them, but the animals remained tense, their eyes fixed on a dense thicket ahead.

"What is it?" one of the men whispered, his knuckles white as he gripped his axe.

He raised a hand, and the others stopped talking. Moving closer to the thicket, Damien's eyes with their augmented sight picked out faint disturbances in the undergrowth. There was the girl's trail still, but something bigger had moved through as well, something which clawed bark on nearby trees.

He knelt, his hand brushing the disturbed ground. Drag marks, no mistake; deeper into the woods they went. The faint sulfurous smell clung in the air now, stronger, like a warning.

"She was taken this way," Damien said, rising to his feet. He glanced back at the group, his expression grim. "Stay together. Whatever did this is still out there."

The men nodded, their grips on the torches and weapons tightening. One of the hounds let out a sharp bark and began tugging at its leash again, anxious to follow the trail.

They trudged on, the lanterns and torches casting a series of eerie, shifting shadows over the forest floor. The rustlings in the trees turned into whispers, loud, faint yet unrelenting, like a chorus of unseen voices entreating them to return wherever they had come.

Vivian walked closer to Damien now, her voice low. "Do you hear that?"

"I do," he returned, his jaw clenching. "Pay it no mind. It's trying to unsettle us."

She nodded, but her fingers strayed to touch the satchel at her side, as if for reassurance from the protecting charms within.

The ground grew softer, almost boggy, underfoot as they walked deeper in. A thin mist started to rise, curling around their ankles like ghostly fingers. The dogs whined softly, huddling, yet kept forward, noses stuck to the earth.

What kind of place is this?" one of the men muttered, his voice shaking. "It feels wrong."

"It is wrong," Damien said, his voice low but steady. "and it's going to get worse. Keep moving."

But even as he spoke, he could feel the weight of Azrathis pressing against his thoughts, its voice slithering through his mind like oil.

"Guardian of men, leading thy small pack of fireflies right into the abyss. Do you really hope to ever find her alive? Or are you marching them into their own graves? Tell me, when it is time, will you actually be strong enough to protect her? Or at last plead with me to do that for you?

Damien pushed the voice aside, forcing himself to focus on the trail ahead. The claw marks were becoming more frequent now, gouges in the trees that oozed a strange, dark sap. The smell of sulfur was almost choking.

"We're getting close," he said grimly. "Stay alert. This isn't just a forest anymore, it's something else entirely."

The men huddled closer, the light from the torches flared against the deepening dark. The dogs whined, their ears laying back along their skull in taut yearning; what lay ahead waited, and it was watching through Damien's eyes out of the dark.

Chapter 7

It was a cathedral of unholy grandeur, its towering walls of obsidian shimmering in living, pulsating light. Veins of crimson luminescence coursed through the darkness like blood coursing through a vein. The floor was not stone but an endless swirl of shadows that seemed to ripple and twist as if the very essence of the Abyss writhed beneath their feet. Overhead, the ceiling disappeared in a sea of darkness, with screams whispering and echoing in the distance, an eternal chorus of torment.

Inside it, an iron table of blackened steel glowed with its engravings and runic writings that ran across its top ablaze with spite and despair. Around this altar of unholy office pressed the most avowed, and dreadest, generals under the power of the Sovereign of Shadows.

At the head sat the Sovereign himself, amorphous dread in the form of a shifting void of darkness that seemed to drink in the faint light of the room. His face was a featureless plane from which two orbs of violet fire burnt, cold and endless, burning into the very soul of anyone that dared gaze upon him. When he spoke, his voice was despair in its purest form, booming within the confines of the chamber as if from a funeral bell.

"We are at the threshold of triumph," the Sovereign began, his words falling like a promise full of venomous intent. "We only need two more children for the ritual. Two fragile lives, and the barrier between our world and the material plane will collapse. When that happens, the Age of Shadows will descend, and the mortals shall be consumed by despair and oblivion."

To his right sat Zephyion, the Shadowblade, a figure of sleek lethality. His pale, angular face seemed carved from alabaster, his black eyes voids of emptiness. Draped in tattered leathers that flickered like smoke, his cursed blade rested across his back, its edges shifting and pulsing as though alive. He leaned forward, his voice a whisper sharp enough to draw blood.

"The mortals grovel in ignorance," Zephyion said, curling his lips in a faint, cruel smile. "The girl they lost is already ours. Her soul screams in the Void, feeding the cracks in the barrier. Two more, and the cage that holds us will shatter. The mortals are pawns, blind to their demise."

Across the table, Lilith the Bloodthirsty laughed, a cruel, jeering sound echoing through the chamber. Her crimson locks cascaded down her bone-plated armor to where her clawed fingers traced lazily along the tabletop as if itching for flesh. In her, her gold eyes flashed with sadistic joy as she spoke.

"Let them pray," she spat, the venom dripping in her words. "Let them plead with their pitiful gods for their salvation. That will make it all the sweeter when we bury their light beneath blood and ashes. Their wails will be my chorus."

"Enough with the theatrics," growled Morgath the Dread-bringer, his deep, guttural voice shaking the chamber. Morgath was a hulking, monstrous figure clad in jagged black armor that seeped a toxic green mist. His spiked helm concealed his face, save for the blazing emerald eyes that burned with rage. "If they dare to resist, I'll crush their armies and break their bones beneath my feet. The weak don't deserve mercy! They deserve annihilation."

"Patience, Morgath," purred Kuloth the Malevolent, his voice cold and calculating. Draped in robes of midnight black, his skeletal fingers steepled before his pale, angular face, Kuloth's presence exuded an aura of suffocating dread. "This isn't a war of brute force alone. When the ritual is complete, they will gladly take the knee. Their minds will break to the weight of our rule, and they shall embrace their own doom."

"Submission is for fools," Azrzel the Infernal hissed, serpentine in form, coiled beside the table, his scales crimson and glistening with reflections of the infernal light; his many fanged smile twisted into the grin of purest malice. "I care not what their minds shall be. Under my claws, it is their bodies that will break, screaming to the Abyss while their flesh feasts my flames. Let Kuloth have their allegiance, and I will savor their agonies."

"Let them fight," rumbled Anthrax the Undying, his decayed, skeletal form looming over the table like death incarnate. His voice was a grinding rasp of stone and bone that sent shivers through the chamber. "Every soul that falls will join my legions. Their resistance is futile. Death is my domain, and they will find no escape from it."

At the far end of the table sat Noctherion the Blackvein, silent and menacing. His towering figure was shrouded in an oozing darkness that seemed to drip like tar. Black veins pulsed beneath his shadowed form, each beat sending waves of oppressive energy through the room. His voice, deep and resonant, was like a star imploding.

"The mortals shall not simply fall," Noctherion intoned, his tone as calm as it was final. "They will become part of the Abyss. Their lands will wither, their skies will blacken, and their light shall be swallowed whole. The material plane will cease to exist as they know it. It will become ours."

The Sovereign lifted his hand, and the murmurs that had followed the naming of Noctherion died instantly. Brighter violet burned within his eyes as he spoke to his generals, the weight of his presence upon them like a storm.

"Zephyion," the Sovereign commanded, "you will lead the final retrieval. The mortals are searching for the girl already. Use their desperation against them. Lure them into our grasp and deliver the remaining two children to me."

Zephyion bowed his head, a sadistic grin spreading across his lips. "It shall be done, my liege. It will be their own hope that proves their undoing."

"Lilith," the Sovereign continued, "summon the Blood Legion. I want it ready to reduce mortal lands to ashes when that gate opens."

Lilith smiled, and in the half-dark, her fangs glittered. "They are already sharpening their blades, my Sovereign. Their hunger knows no limits."

The Sovereign perpetrated his will by standing from his throne, and his shadow opened like a living thing, pouring into the chamber an unbreathable darkness. "Go now, my generals. Prepare for the final step. When the gate opens, the material plane shall burn, and the Age of Shadows will consume all."

The generals bowed one by one, tattered into the dark like smoke into the Abyss. He alone, the Sovereign, remained standing there, his eyes fixed upon the churning shadows before him, his eyes burning with fire.

"Soon," he breathed, his voice full of malice. "The mortals shall fall on their knees, their gods silenced, and the world plunged into eternal night."

<h1 style="text-align:center">Chapter 8</h1>

It would have seemed that time froze the party of searchers, the glowing sigil below their feet casting its unnatural, crimson light dancing upon their pale features. The air was heavy with weight, thick with malice and the faint, acrid scent of sulfur.

He looked around at the group, their fear etched in every nervous glance and trembling hand. The longer they stayed, the more dangerous it was for them, and the easier it would be for the Sovereign's influence to take hold.

"Everyone," Damien said, his voice firm, cutting through the heavy silence. "This place is dangerous. I need you all to leave and return to the village. Tell the Rabbi what we've found here, but do not come back. I'll stay and study the mark. Whatever this is, it's not something you need to face."

A murmur rippled through the crowd, and one of them stepped forward, his grasp on the handle of his torch tightening. "But Damien," he began stumblingly, "what if. what if you need us? What if it tries to—"

"I will be fine," Damien cut in, his voice brooking no further argument. "You've seen what this place can do. To stay here puts all of you in greater danger. I will return to the village when I know more."

The villagers exchanged uneasy glances, reluctant to leave him behind, but Damien's unwavering expression left little room for debate. Slowly, one by one, they began to retreat, their torches bobbing like faint stars as they disappeared into the oppressive darkness of the forest.

Only Vivian remained, her green eyes locked on Damien, worry etched into her features. "You're staying here alone?" she asked, her voice quiet but tense.

"I have to," Damien said. "Whatever this is, it's connected with the children. If we can comprehend its purpose, we may have a way of stopping the ritual. But I also need you to go back."

She scowled, protesting, but before she could get a word out, Damien forged ahead. "I need you to round up supplies: gloves, vials, protective charms. Bring anything that we can use to take samples of this safely. Bring them back here, and we'll work together to figure out what this mark is and how to counteract it."

Vivian hesitated, her hands tightening on the strap of her satchel. "Damien. what if something happens while I'm gone? This place feels alive. It's watching us."

He stepped closer, his expression softening. "I'll be fine," he said, lowering his voice. "You know me better than that."

She nodded reluctantly, though her eyes lingered on the glowing sigil as if it might lash out at any moment. "I'll be quick," she said finally, her voice firm despite the fear in her expression. "Don't do anything reckless."

As Vivian turned and vanished into the darkness, Damien was left alone in the clearing. The sigil pulsed faintly, its jagged lines dancing with an otherworldly light. The weight of the energy seemed to press in a little harder without her, as if the mark in the earth itself had been waiting for solitude.

"That was foolish, mortal," came the insidious voice of Xandros, curling through his thoughts like smoke. "Sending them away? They could have been useful. Fodder, if nothing else."

Damien gave the demon no great heed, went directly to sit on his knees on one side of the sigil, and bent into a deep study of it: deeply engraved into the ground he whispered between his teeth, "This isn't any regular summoning sign," his fingers hovering gloved over skin searing heat shimmering up from blistering earth.

"You can feel it, can't you?" Azrathis hissed, his tone both mocking and tempting. "The power it emits, the connection it makes. This is a gateway, mortal. A door between realms. It's incomplete, and they're still waiting for the final keys to open it."

His jaw clenched as Damien finally sketched the sigil in his journal, noting every jagged rune and glowing line. He could feel the weight of the Sovereign's power emanating from the mark, sending a shiver through the air with each pulse.

The sigil flared brighter in an instant, casting long, twisted shadows across the clearing. The air grew colder, heavy with unnatural stillness. A low, guttural voice rose from the center of the mark, its tone dripping with malice.

"You should not have stayed."

Damien stood, sword drawn, his eyes locked on the sigil as the voice continued.

"You think you can stop what is coming? You are nothing. A speck of light waiting to be snuffed out. The Sovereign sees you, mortal, and he laughs at your defiance." Damian clenched his fist on the hilt of his sword; the blade gleamed faintly in the crimson glow. "Tell your Sovereign he won't have this world," he said, his voice low and even. "Not while I still draw breath.

The voice exploded into a deep, mirthless laugh that echoed through the clearing. "Your breath means nothing. Your strength means nothing. The gate shall open, and your precious world will drown in shadow."

As the sigil's glow once more began to dim, Damien exhaled slowly before loosening his grip upon his sword. The Sovereign's taunt still lingered within the air, the cold whisper of a combat to be joined.

He knelt once more and continued his drawings and notes. If there was some method of interference for the mark, he would find it. The world, literally, and the lost children depended on his unburdened shoulders.

The forest was silent, but Damien knew the abyss stared back with unseen eyes. He tried to shake off the chill creeping down his spine, refocusing harder than ever on his work, to understand the secrets the sigil held before it would be too late.

The search party was long gone, their torches consumed by the heavy darkness of the forest. Only Damien remained, standing sentinel over the glowing sigil that had been burnt into the earth. The faint crimson light cast long, shifting shadows dancing at the edge of his vision to taunt him. He knelt again, tracing in his journal the jagged lines of the mark, every stroke deliberate.

The air seemed thicker now, pressing against his chest as though the very forest sought to smother him. Azrathis's voice whispered through his mind, its presence heavier in the silence.

"You feel it, don't you? Time bends here. Space twists. You're already losing yourself. That is the Sovereign's domain creeping into your fragile little world."

Damien's jaw clenched, silent and unyielding to the demon's words. He returned to his task, writing down every detail of the sigil. Its power disoriented him; its pulse was a strange cadence, dragging time slower, thinner, like molasses into the abyss.

The crunching of leaves in the distance snapped him out of his trance. He whirled, sword in hand, as a figure emerged from the shadows.

"Damien?" Vivian's breathless voice came through with a steady calmness as she stepped into the clearing with a satchel full of provisions slung over her shoulder. Her lantern cast a soft glow across her face; her cheeks had a flush from the exertion.

"Vivian?" Damien's brow furrowed as he lowered his sword. "You're already back? You were gone for what, five minutes?"

Her face changed to puzzlement as she stopped a few feet away from him, her chest heaving up and down in the quick rush to get back. "Five minutes? Damien, I was gone for almost forty-five. I ran back as fast as possible with everything we might need."

The sudden words were sinking in, and his hand gripped tighter on the hilt of his sword. "Forty-five minutes?" he repeated out loud with a look toward the sigil and then back to her. "That's not possible."

Vivian's lips pressed into a thin line as she opened the satchel and she pulled out the requested items—vials, gloves, and several small charms designed to ward against demonic energy. "It is possible," she said. "Time moves differently here, Damien.

You've felt it, haven't you? That heaviness, the way everything slows down. Whatever this mark is, it's warping more than just the forest."

He snorted loudly and raked a hand through his hair. "I thought it was just the atmosphere, the Sovereign's influence weighing on us. But this—" He gestured at the sigil, its faint glow pulsated in an almost hypnotic rhythm. "This is worse than I thought."

Vivian dropped down beside him and handed him another pair of gloves. "There is no time to debate what is going on. If the mark of the Sovereign distorted time, it means whatever he has planned has accelerated. We need to find out how to stop it."

Damien nodded, putting on the gloves and reaching carefully for the edge of the sigil. It was hotter now like the mark could sense their presence and was reacting to their intrusion. "Did you bring something to store the samples?"

Vivian pulled out a set of small, reinforced vials. "Here," she said, handing them to him. "These should contain whatever energy or residue this thing gives off. Just be careful. It feels alive."

"Alive. One word to describe it." Damien muttered, dropping into a crouch closer to the sigil. He held one of the vials a hair above the surface and peered inside, watching the faint, smoky essence of his summoning start to swirl within the container. It vibrated very faintly in his hand, apparently unwilling.

Vivian watched him work, her fingers brushing one of the protective charms hanging from her belt. "Damien," she said softly, "when I was running back, I kept hearing things. Whispers in the trees. I tried to block them out, but it was like they were following me."

His gaze flickered to her momentarily before returning to the sigil. "The Sovereign's reach," he said. "It's growing. He wants us to feel his presence, to break our focus. Don't let it get to you."

Vivian shivered but nodded. "What do you think he's planning, Damien? The children, the sigils, what's the endgame here?"

Damien sealed the vial with a sharp motion, his jaw tightening. "If I'm right, these sigils are part of a larger ritual. He's trying to weaken the barrier between his realm and ours. Once it falls." He trailed off, his expression darkening.

Vivian swallowed hard. "Once it falls, he'll invade."

"Precisely," Damien said, reaching for another vial as his careful collection of the essence of the sigil continued. "That's why we need to hurry. Every minute we waste brings him closer to opening that gate."

The flaring of the sigil brightened for a moment, casting an eerie red glow over the clearing. They both froze as a faint whisper, a child's voice, called for help out of the trees.

Vivian's eyes darted toward the sound. "Did you hear that?"

Damien's grip on the vial tightened, and his voice came low and level. "It's not her. It's a lure. Don't fall for it."

She nodded, though her hands were shaking a little as she clutched her satchel closer. The oppressive energy of the sigil seemed to throb louder, and Damien felt the voice of Azrathis stirred in his mind.

"Ah, mortal, do you feel it now? The Sovereign's grip grows stronger, his whispers closer. You stand in the jaws of the abyss and yet you still resist. How much longer before you fall? How much longer before you beg me to help you?"

Damien clamped his teeth down, cramming the voice deep

inside his brain. He rose, holding the sealed vials up. "We have what we need for the time being," he said, voice steady. "Let's go back to the village and plan our next step. This place is stirring, and we must not be here when it comes alive."

She nodded, and the fear in her eyes gave way to determination. As they started their retreat from the clearing, Damien spoke once more, this time with his voice quiet but resolute. "We need to find the counter sigil," he said. "If this is a gateway, there has to be a way to seal it. A mark to close what's been opened."

Vivian cast a look his way, her expression taut. "And you're sure you can find it?"

"I have to," Damien replied. "But there's something else I need to do first. I need to speak with the Dean about the upcoming class. There's no room for mistakes—not with what's at stake."

Vivian frowned but said nothing, and she followed him silently as they made their way back toward the village. Behind them, the sigil pulsed faintly in the darkness, a malevolent promise of the Sovereign's encroaching power.

Chapter 9

The halls of the university were quieter than usual, the faint echoes of Damien's boots the only sound as he made his way to the Dean's office. The weight of the sigil he had encountered in the forest lingered in his mind, but he forced himself to focus. This was important because he could control the chaos creeping into the world.

The heavy oak door to Dean Valcroft's office was ajar, a faint golden light spilling into the corridor. Damien knocked twice before stepping inside, his satchel of documents clutched in one hand.

The office was as daunting as ever: thick with the scent of old parchment and a faint tinge of incense. A bank of lines up to the ceiling stood tall in a stretch of bookshelves, and in the center of the room was a grand oaken desk occupied by the Dean himself, with scribbled notes on parchment. He looked up at the entrance of Damien, sharp eyes narrowing with curiosity.

"Damien," Valcroft said, laying his quill aside. "I wasn't expecting you quite so early. Something on your mind?"

Damien inclined his head. "Yes, Dean. I wanted to discuss Introduction to Religion and Occultism. I've worked out a proposal on how I would like to structure the class, and I believe it will meet, perhaps exceed, the university's expectations."

The Dean motioned for him to go on, reclining back in his chair as Damien stepped to the desk and laid a neatly bound document before him.

"This course," Damien began, "is essential for students pursuing degrees in Religious Studies, International Business, and Industrial Welfare. It provides them with a foundational understanding of the world's major religions and the occult movements that are rising in prominence. To ensure the information is delivered accurately and respectfully, I've structured it so that experts from each faith will handle their respective sections."

The Dean had raised an eyebrow, and he could tell he was intrigued. "Experts?"

Damien nodded. "A rabbi to teach Judaism, a nun to teach Catholicism, and an Islamic scholar to teach Islam. They will teach their respective sections, ensuring that their material is not only accurate but also presented in a manner acceptable to each of those faiths."

Valcroft stroked his beard thoughtfully. "And the occult section?

"I'll take care of that myself," Damien said. "It's a pretty sensitive topic, and I want to ensure it's approached objectively. I don't want to sensationalize or trivialize it, but rather let the students know what was happening so they can understand the historical and social ramifications."

The Dean flipped through the course outline, his sharp gaze scanning the headings. Week 1: Introduction to Religion and

Occultism, Weeks 2–3: Catholicism, Weeks 4–5: Judaism, Weeks 6–7: Islam, Weeks 8–9: Occultism, Weeks 10–11: Reflection, Interfaith Dialogue, and Exams.

"I'll begin the course with an introduction," Damien continued, "providing a framework for understanding religion and occultism in a historical and cultural context. This will allow the guest instructors to delve into their respective areas. At the end of the course, I'll lead a concluding session that brings all the sections together, fostering interfaith dialogue and encouraging students to reflect on what they've learned."

Valcroft leaned back in his chair, fingers steepled. "You have put considerable thought into this, Damien. Bringing in practitioners from each faith is an inspired idea, one that lends both credibility and balance to the material."

Damien nodded. "Thanks, Dean. Religion is a very personal thing, and I'd like to make sure we respect that. Having practitioners teach their traditions will give us authenticity and it will prove the merit of interfaith collaboration."

"And you already have people in mind, I presume?" the Dean asked.

"Yes," Damien said. "For Judaism, Rabbi Eliezer Stern. A scholar of Jewish history and theology, he is also highly noted for teaching competence. For Catholicism, Sister Marian Lourdes has both academic and pastoral experience from her ministerial works. And for Islam, Imam Khalid Al-Rahman, whose lectures are reputed for clarity and depth." The Dean nodded in approval. "Solid choices. And how do you propose to coordinate their efforts?"

"They'll each handle their sections independently," Damien explained, "but during the final weeks, I'll bring them together for a panel discussion. This will allow students to see how these faiths intersect, where they diverge, and how they've shaped society. It will also encourage critical thinking and dialogue among the students."

Valcroft's lips arced into a faint smile. "Ambitious, Damien. I like it. This course could be much more than an education for the students; it can challenge their view of the world in a broader perspective.

Damien leaned forward slightly, his voice firm. "That's exactly what we need. In today's fractured world, understanding faith, both its power and its pitfalls is crucial. If we fail to teach this properly, we risk leaving our students unprepared for the complexities they'll face."

The Dean stared at him a moment before nodding. "Alright then. I grant this format. Contact your participants and prepare things. I need this all taken care of prior to the semester kicking in."

"Thanks, Dean," Damien said, coming forward with his hand outstretched. "I will not leave one stone unturned."

Satchel lighter but mind burdened by the same thoughts of that sigil deep in the woods and a rising Sovereign force, Damien had little else running in his head but how such knowledge was literally mankind's deadliest sword. "The counter sigil needs to be discovered now, and to see this class is developed specifically to give it what it wants," Damien said to himself.

Chapter 10

Damien's study was cloaked in an uneasy stillness, the faint crackle of the lantern casting flickering shadows across the room. The scent of old parchment and ink filled the air, mingling with the faint sulfuric tang that seemed to follow him since his encounter with the sigil. On his desk lay his journal, open to the page where he had meticulously sketched the mark of the Sovereign, its jagged lines glaring back at him like a taunt.

He leaned back in his chair, staring at the sigil's twisted design. There were no answers here—not in his books, not in the rituals he had studied. The Sovereign's power was something far beyond the mortal realm, and the forces he had at his command were relentless. Damien knew this was a fight he couldn't win alone.

"You're starting to see it, aren't you?"

The voice came, slithering through his mind like a shadow creeping beneath a door. It was dark, low, and laced with the familiar blend of mockery and menace.

Damien's grip on the desk tightened. "I don't have time for your games," he muttered, his voice low but sharp.

The demon laughed, its voice a deep, guttural rumble that reverberated through his thoughts. "Oh, Damien, but you do. Because you're at the end of your rope, aren't you? You've searched every text, scoured every ritual, and you're still empty-handed. Face it, you need me."

Damien stood abruptly, pacing the length of the room. The shadows cast by the lantern seemed to warp and stretch as he moved, twisting unnaturally as if alive. "Why would I ever trust you?" he snapped, his voice rising. "You're trapped in me, bound by the amulet. Everything you say, everything you offer, is for your own benefit."

"And yet I'm here," the demon replied smoothly, its tone shifting to something almost coaxing. "I could remain silent, Damien. I could sit in the dark corners of your mind, waiting for the day you finally crumble under the weight of all this. But I don't. Because despite what you think, I have no interest in seeing you fail."

Damien turned sharply toward the desk, his dark eyes narrowing. "No interest? You're bound to me because of the amulet. You don't have a choice but to stay. Don't try to pretend this is altruism."

The demon chuckled, low and insidious. "True, the amulet binds me to you. But don't think that makes you my master. This isn't a leash, Damien. It's a cage. Moreover, while I might be stuck with you, that doesn't mean I'm powerless. If I wanted to, I could whisper poison into your thoughts, cloud your judgment, and make you question everything you know. But instead… I'm offering you something you can't refuse."

Damien crossed his arms, his voice hard. "And what's that?"

"Knowledge," the demon hissed, its voice dripping with malice and promise. "Insight into the Sovereign and his generals. Their weaknesses. Their desires. I've seen their kind before, Damien. I know how they think and how they plan. You're walking into a war you don't understand, but with me? You might just survive it."

Damien paused, his jaw tightening. He hated how tempting the words were. The Sovereign's power was vast, and his generals were creatures of unimaginable malice and cunning. If the demon truly knew how to fight them, then…

"No," Damien said finally, his voice firm. "I'm not making a deal with you. Every offer you make comes with a price. I've spent my life keeping demons like you in check. Why should I believe you won't twist this to your advantage?"

"Oh, Damien," the demon murmured, its tone turning darker, more insidious. "You think you're in control, don't you? That little amulet of yours might keep me bound, but it doesn't make you invincible. You've used me before, whether you want to admit it or not. In the woods, remember? It was my gift that let you see through the darkness, which saved your precious search party. Without me, you'd have stumbled blindly to your death."

Damien clenched his fists, the truth of the words stinging more than he cared to admit. "That doesn't mean I trust you."

"You don't have to trust me," the demon replied smoothly. "But you do have to use me. You're fighting something far greater than you, a Sovereign with legions of loyal generals and centuries of malice behind him. You think your sword and your books will be enough? You'll fail, Damien. And when you do, they'll burn this world to ash."

Damien turned back to the desk, staring down at the sigil he had sketched. His mind churned with the weight of the decision before him. He hated the idea of relying on the demon, but he couldn't deny the truth: he was outmatched.

"And what's your price?" he asked finally, his voice low.

The demon laughed again, but this time, it was softer, more sinister. "Oh, Damien, my price is simple. When this is over, when the Sovereign is defeated, and his generals are no more, you'll remove the amulet. You'll release me. That's all I ask. Freedom for the knowledge you so desperately need."

Damien's eyes narrowed. "And you expect me to believe you'll just leave? That you won't wreak havoc the moment you're free?"

"What havoc could I cause?" the demon asked, its tone almost amused. "There are far grander games for me to play than meddling in your little mortal world. All I want is my freedom, Damien. You have my word, take it or leave it."

Silence fell over the room, the lantern's faint crackle the only sound. Damien's mind raced, weighing the risks and the potential benefits. The demon was bound to him by the amulet, but even so, it had proven useful. If it truly had knowledge of the Sovereign and his generals, then perhaps…

Finally, he spoke, his voice hard and resolute. "Fine. I'll accept your help. But on my terms. You give me everything I need to stop the Sovereign and protect this world. And if, IF, we succeed, I'll consider releasing you."

The demon's voice deepened, a dark, menacing rumble that seemed to vibrate through the room. "Oh, Damien, you've just made a dangerous choice. But I'll accept. You'll have my knowledge, my guidance. Together, we'll tear the Sovereign and his generals apart. But remember this: every step you take with me brings you closer to becoming what you fear most."

The words hung in the air, heavy with foreboding. Damien exhaled slowly, his fists unclenching as he sat back down.

"Then let's begin," he said, his voice steady. "Tell me about the Sovereign's generals. If you're so eager to help, start talking."

The demon chuckled, its tone almost eager. "Oh, Damien, you're going to enjoy this. Let's start with Zephyion, the Shadowblade. Cunning, ruthless… and dangerously predictable. He'll be the first to fall."

As the demon began to weave its dark knowledge, Damien felt the weight of his decision settle over him like a shadow. He didn't trust the creature, he never would, but for now, it was a weapon he couldn't afford to discard.

And he would wield it carefully, knowing that the blade cut both ways.

Chapter 11

Damien sat amidst the dying light in his study, the lantern's fire dancing little more than a feeble bulwark against the heavy shadows that crept closer with every passing moment. It was a smaller room now, and it felt as if the walls themselves leaned in to listen. Before him on the desk lay his journal, open to the jagged sketch of the Sovereign's sigil. The lines, once still, now seemed to pulse faintly in the lamplight, mocking him.

"Let's talk strategy, mortal," the demon's voice slithered into his mind, smooth and insidious. "You have already wasted too much time fumbling in the dark. Let me shed some light on things for you."

Damien exhaled sharply, his hand tightening into a fist on the desk. "Fine," he muttered. "Talk.

The demon's laughter rumbled low, a sound that felt like it came from the walls themselves. "Good boy. Now, listen closely. The Sovereign's power is vast, but he doesn't wield it alone. His generals are the foundation of his strength, each of them representing a piece of his influence. To cripple him, you have to dismantle them first."

Damien jerked a new page in his journal and scribbled a hasty note. "Who's the weakest?"

"Zephyion, the Shadowblade," the demon replied, its voice sharpening. "He's ruthless and cunning but arrogant. He relies too much on his speed and his blade. He'll assume you're just another mortal to cut down, but we can use that. His pride is his greatest weakness."

Damien nodded, jotting down the demon's words. "And the others?"

"Ah, the others," the demon purred, its voice falling darker. "Morgath, the Dreadbringe, he's brute force incarnate. He'll tear through anything in his path, but he's predictable. Then there's Kuloth, the Malevolent. Watch him closely, Damien. He's cunning he moves pieces on a board you can't even see. And don't forget Azrzel, Anthrax, Lilith. and Noctherion."

The demon's voice seemed to linger on the last name, and a shiver ran down Damien's spine.

"Noctherion," Damien repeated, his pen pausing. "Why does that name sound different?

"Because he's not like the others," the demon hissed, its voice dipping into a sinister growl. "He's not just a general, he's the Sovereign's anchor. Without him, the Sovereign's power in your world will falter. But mark my words, Damien, Noctherion will be the hardest to bring down. You'll need every ounce of strength, every trick, every ally. and, of course, me."

Damien leaned back in his chair, his jaw tight. "You're enjoying this, aren't you?"

"Immensely," the demon admitted with a chuckle. "But don't confuse enjoyment with frivolity. I want the Sovereign gone as much as you do. He's a threat to me as much as he is to you. Help me destroy him, and we both walk away free."

Damien's eyes flicked to the amulet hanging from a chain around his neck, hidden beneath his shirt. Its faint weight was a constant reminder of the curse binding the demon to him. He didn't trust it, and he never would, but he couldn't deny the value of its insight.

"Fine," he said finally. "We take down Zephyion first. Tell me what I need to know."

"Ah, now you're thinking like a hunter," the demon said, its voice curling with satisfaction. "Zephyion thrives in shadows, but he's impatient. Lure him out, make him think he has the upper hand, and strike when he overcommits. But first, you'll need a proper weapon, something that can cut through his defenses. His blade isn't just steel, you know. It's shadow-forged, and no ordinary sword will stand against it."

Damien wrote furiously, the words of the demon flaring into a plan in his head. "And where am I to find this?"

"Oh, I'll tell you," the demon purred, its voice low, almost teasing. "But not tonight. You're not ready yet. First, you will have to deal with what's already burgeoning inside you."

Damien stilled, his pen hesitating over the paper. "What are you talking about?

The demon's laughter returned, softer this time, yet no less sinister. "Oh, Damien, did you really think there was not a price to pay? No side effects? You have tapped into my power and used it to see in the dark, to survive when others would have fallen. But power always leaves its mark."

Damien's frown deepened; his pulse quickened. He pushed back from the desk and rose, striding to the mirror on the far wall. The dim light of the lantern reflected his face, pale but familiar.

And then he saw it.

A faint shadow flickered in the back of his eyes, a darkness seeming to twist and ripple like smoke. He bent closer, digging his fingers into the edges of the mirror. The shadow took on more definition, coiling through his pupils before dissipating as quickly as it had appeared.

"What. what is that?" he whispered, his voice barely audible.

"A sign," the demon said, his voice low, almost amused. "My power is seeping into you, Damien. You opened the door when you took my sight, and now it's leaving its trace. The amulet binds me, yes, but every time you use me, every time you draw on what I can give you, the bond between us deepens."

The room seemed to shrink as Damien's chest tightened. His hand instinctively went to the amulet beneath his shirt. It was warm against his skin, almost uncomfortably so.

"Is it permanent?" he asked, his voice sharp.

"Not yet," the demon said. "But the more you rely on me, the more connected we'll become. Think of it as a partnership, Damien. The more you take, the more I'll leave behind. But don't fret, and I'll make sure you're still useful when this is over."

Damien clenched his jaw, his fist clenching into the chain of the amulet. "If you're lying to me—"

"Oh, I am not lying," the demon cut in, his voice a silken whisper. "Why would I? I want you alive, Damien. Alive, strong, and only desperate enough to make use of what I offer. Now, shall we continue or would you rather stare at the darkness growing in your soul a little longer?"

Damien forced his grip to loosen, letting the air seep slowly from his lungs. He turned back to the desk, and his mind raced. He hated the demon, hated the way its words wrapped around his thoughts like chains, but he couldn't deny the truth.

"Fine," he muttered, sitting down again. "We keep going. But if you push me too far, I'll find a way to bury you deeper than you've ever been."

"Oh, Damien," the demon purred, his voice oozing with malice. "You keep saying that. But we know you'll use me again. And again. Until the line between us isn't so clear anymore."

The lantern flickered, the shadows in the room seeming to twist closer. Damien ignored the chill that ran down his spine and focused on his notes. Whatever the cost, whatever the risk, he would stop the Sovereign.

The laughter of the demon still echoed at the back of his mind, a constant reminder of the danger inside him.

About the Author

Lee Alexander is a fantasy and Gothic horror author known for crafting immersive narratives that blend supernatural intrigue with rich world-building. His debut novella, Shadows of the Past: The Damien Blackwell Chronicles, introduced readers to a chilling tale of dark secrets and eerie mysteries, marking the beginning of a gripping four-book series. The saga continues with Echoes of Shadow and Light, further unraveling the dark past and haunting forces that shape Damien Blackwell's fate.

In addition to Gothic horror, Lee's fantasy novel The Fortuitous Few transports readers into a richly detailed world inspired by his decades of experience as a Dungeon Master. Featuring a diverse cast of adventurers, this tale weaves high-stakes adventure with deep character-driven storytelling.

A strong advocate for intellectual freedom, Lee is an active member of author and publishing organizations that oppose book bans and censorship. His work champions the power of storytelling in its raw, unfiltered form.

Follow his latest works on Instagram: @leea.writes or contact him at leealexander.writes@gmail.com.